BABYMOUSE
QUEEN OF THE WORLD!

BY JENNIFER L. HOLM & MATTHEW HOLM

HarperCollins *Children's Books*

First published in the U.S.A. by Random House Children's Books in 2005
First published in paperback in Great Britain by HarperCollins Children's Books in 2006

1 3 5 7 9 10 8 6 4 2
ISBN-13: 978-0-00-722447-0
ISBN-10: 0-00-722447-8

HarperCollins Children's books is a division of HarperCollins Publishers Ltd.

Text and illustrations copyright © Jennifer Holm and Matthew Holm 2005

RINGG!

RINNGGG!!!

FWAP!

IT WAS THE SAME THING EVERY DAY FOR BABYMOUSE.

WAKE UP.

ALL BABYMOUSE HAD WAS AN OVERDUE LIBRARY BOOK AND A LOCKER THAT STUCK.

NNNGGHH!

IT WAS JUST ONE MORE THING
SHE WAS STUCK WITH.

13

STUCK WITH WASTE REMOVAL DUTIES.

BABYMOUSE, WOULD YOU MIND TAKING OUT THE RUBBISH?

STUCK WITH AN ANNOYING LITTLE BROTHER.

LET GO, SQUEAK!

TUG

TUG

STUCK WITH HOMEWORK.

DRAGONS
WILD WEST
FAIRY TALES
DETECTIVES
SPOOKY
WOW!
FUN

GRAMMAR-RAMA
YAWN
DULL HISTORY
FRACTIONS

COOL BOOKS TO READ

BORING HOMEWORK TO DO

STUCK WITH CURLY WHISKERS.

ARRGGHH!!

BABYMOUSE DIDN'T HAVE A LOT OF EXPECTATIONS.

HMMM...

WELL, MAYBE JUST A FEW.
TIARA!
ICE CREAM FOR LUNCH!
STRAIGHT WHISKERS!
NO HOMEWORK!
QUEEN OF THE WORLD!

, HI THERE, FELICIA, HOW ARE YOU TODAY? I HEARD
-VI... ...I FOR LUNCH TODAY. ISN'T THAT
REA... ...G'S BETTER THAN THAT MEAT
HE... ...E. YUCK! I WONDER IF IT EVEN HA
EA... ...ONALLY, I DON'T REALLY LIKE ANY
HA... ...RD "LOAF" IN IT. WELL, EXCEPT B
HOO... ...T COUNT? I GUESS NOT. OH — AND
HAT... ...HE NEATEST BOOK, ABOUT THI
HO... ...S A WIZARD AND GETS TO GO TO
OOL... ...OOL. ISN'T THAT COOL? I WISH WE
O A... ...OL. THEN WE COULD LEARN TO DO
HD... ...STUFF INSTEAD OF HAVING TO L
BOO... ...CTIONS. FELICIA, W... ...OU LIK

OKAY...
BE COOL...

FRIDAY NIGHT. MY HOUSE. ATTACK OF THE GIANT SQUID.

COOL!

RINNGG!!

SEE YOU IN CLASS.

I LOVE MONSTER MOVIES.

SPOOKY FOG.

SSSSSSS...

CLICK!

HEY! WHO TURNED OUT THE LIGHTS?

THIS IS KIND OF SPOOKY.

WHAT WAS THAT?

TAP TAP

AAAGGHH!!

Her straight whiskers should have tipped me off that she was trouble.

SNEAKY EYES

STRAIGHT WHISKERS

COOL SHOES

But in my line of work, you see it all.

LUNCHTIME...WHERE THE FOOD WAS DEFINITELY NOT FIT FOR A QUEEN – OR EVEN AN ASSISTANT QUEEN.

EWW.

MEATLOAF AGAIN? BLEAH!

PLOP!

NOT TO MENTION, SOMEONE WAS SITTING ON BABYMOUSE'S THRONE.

THERE'S NO ROOM, BABYMOUSE.

TYPICAL.

WHERE'S A PRINCE WHEN YOU NEED HIM, ANYWAY?

OVER HERE, BABYMOUSE! I SAVED YOU A SEAT.

POOR BABYMOUSERELLA.

BABYMOUSE SURE COULD USE A LITTLE HELP HERE.

34

TRANSPORTATION HAD BEEN ARRANGED.

A BANANA?

THEY WERE OUT OF PUMPKINS.

THERE WAS ONE SMALL PROBLEM, THOUGH.

CLICK

HEY! GET OUT OF MY CARRIAGE!

YOUR CARRIAGE? THIS IS MY CARRIAGE. YOU'RE PULLING IT!

WHAT?!

IT SEEMED LIKE EVERYONE WAS INVITED TO THE SLEEPOVER PARTY.

BABYMOUSE KNEW THE SLEEPOVER PARTY WAS HER BIG CHANCE TO SHOW FELICIA FURRYPAWS HOW COOL SHE WAS!

SHE COULD SEE IT NOW.

PLEASE SAY YOU'LL BE MY BEST FRIEND.

I SUPPOSE.

...WHICH IS WHY MICE EAT CHEESE!

HA HA HA HA HA HA HA HA HA HA HA HA HA

I NEVER KNEW HOW COOL SHE WAS!

HER WHOLE LIFE WOULD BE DIFFERENT.

CAN I BORROW YOUR DRESS SOMETIME? THE HEART IS SO STYLISH!

I KNOW.

HOW DO YOU GET YOUR WHISKERS SO CURLY?

THEY'RE NATURAL.

DEEP SPACE.

44

THE LIFE OF A SPACE EXPLORER WAS A LONELY ONE.

45

THEY DARED NOT FAIL.

THERE IT IS, CAPTAIN!

FINALLY, AFTER ALL THESE YEARS...

WE'VE FOUND WHAT WE'VE SEARCHED THE GALAXY FOR!

ALIEN LIFE, CAPTAIN?

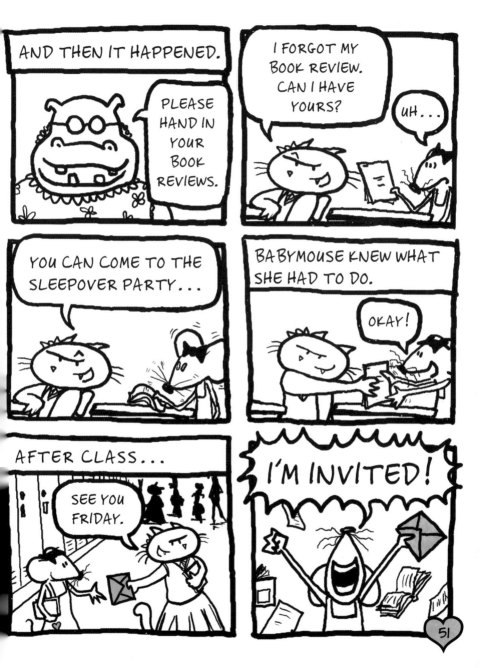

I'M INVITED! I'M INVITED! I'M INVITED! I'M INVITED! I -

UH-OH. LOOKS LIKE BABYMOUSE IS IN TROUBLE.

BABYMOUSE, CAN I SPEAK TO YOU ABOUT YOUR BOOK REVIEW?

GULP!

I THOUGHT YOU DID YOUR BOOK REVIEW...

I, UH, GUESS I FORGOT.

NOTE FROM TEACHER

MUM, CAN I GO TO FELICIA FURRYPAWS' SLEEPOVER PARTY FRIDAY NIGHT?

WELL...

BOUNCE

BOUNCE

WHOOSH!

THANKS!

BABYMOUSE DECIDED TO PACK RIGHT AWAY!

ON

GO

CREEAAK...

RRRUUMMBBLE!

BABYMOUSE KNEW THE SLEEPOVER PARTY WOULD BE A GLAMOROUS EVENT.

NOW, WHAT SHOULD I BRING?

SHE HAD TO FIND THE PERFECT OUTFIT.

HMM...

BABYMOUSE WAS EXCITED THE WHOLE WAY OVER TO FELICIA'S.

SHE HAD LOTS OF IDEAS ABOUT WHAT THEY WERE GOING TO DO.

SKYDIVING!

THEATRE!

GO-KART RACING!

SNORKELLING!

WILD "BABY" MOUSE!

DRIP
DRIZZLE
DRIZZLE

I will love you forever, Lara. *SMOOCH*

AWWWW!!!!

THAT WAS THE BEST MOVIE EVER!

I WONDER IF WILSON IS WATCHING MONSTER MOVIES.

DID YOU SEE GEORGIE THE GIRAFFE THROW UP AFTER LUNCH? HE IS SO GROSS! AND HIS NECK IS CROOKED!

HA HA HA HA HA HA HA HA!

CRACK!!

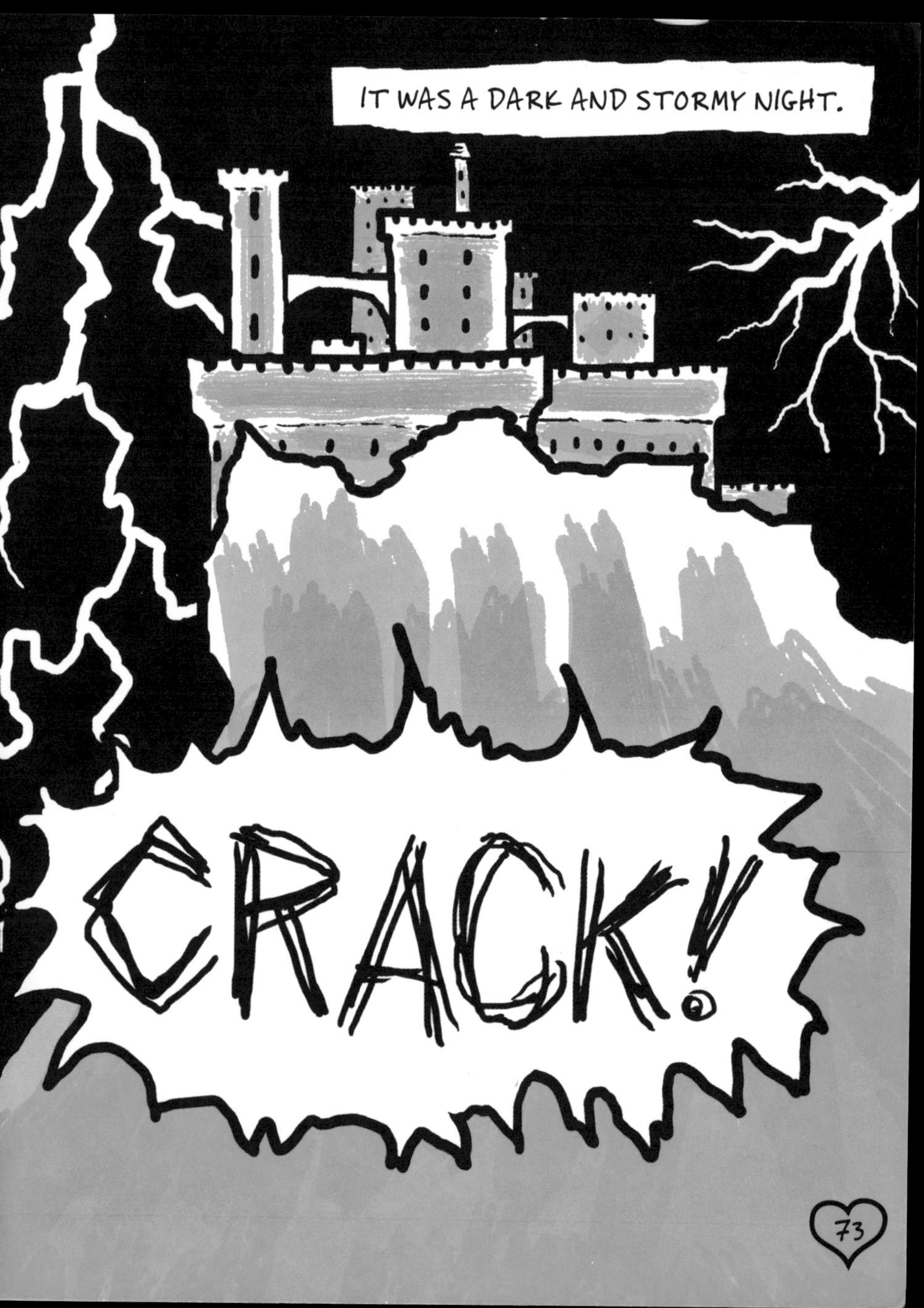
IT WAS A DARK AND STORMY NIGHT.
CRACK!

LADY BABYMOUSE HAD COME TO CASTLE WEASELSTEIN.

IT WAS SAID THAT DR. WEASELSTEIN CONDUCTED STRANGE EXPERIMENTS IN HIS TOWER LABORATORY.

SOME SPOKE OF A MONSTER.

BUT LADY BABYMOUSE WAS NOT FAINT OF HEART.

AND WILSON THE WEASEL IS SUCH A DOOFUS.

POP

HA HA HA HA HA HA HA HA!

OH NO!

WHAT HAD SHE DONE?

I GUESS BABYMOUSE FOUND ANOTHER BEST FRIEND.

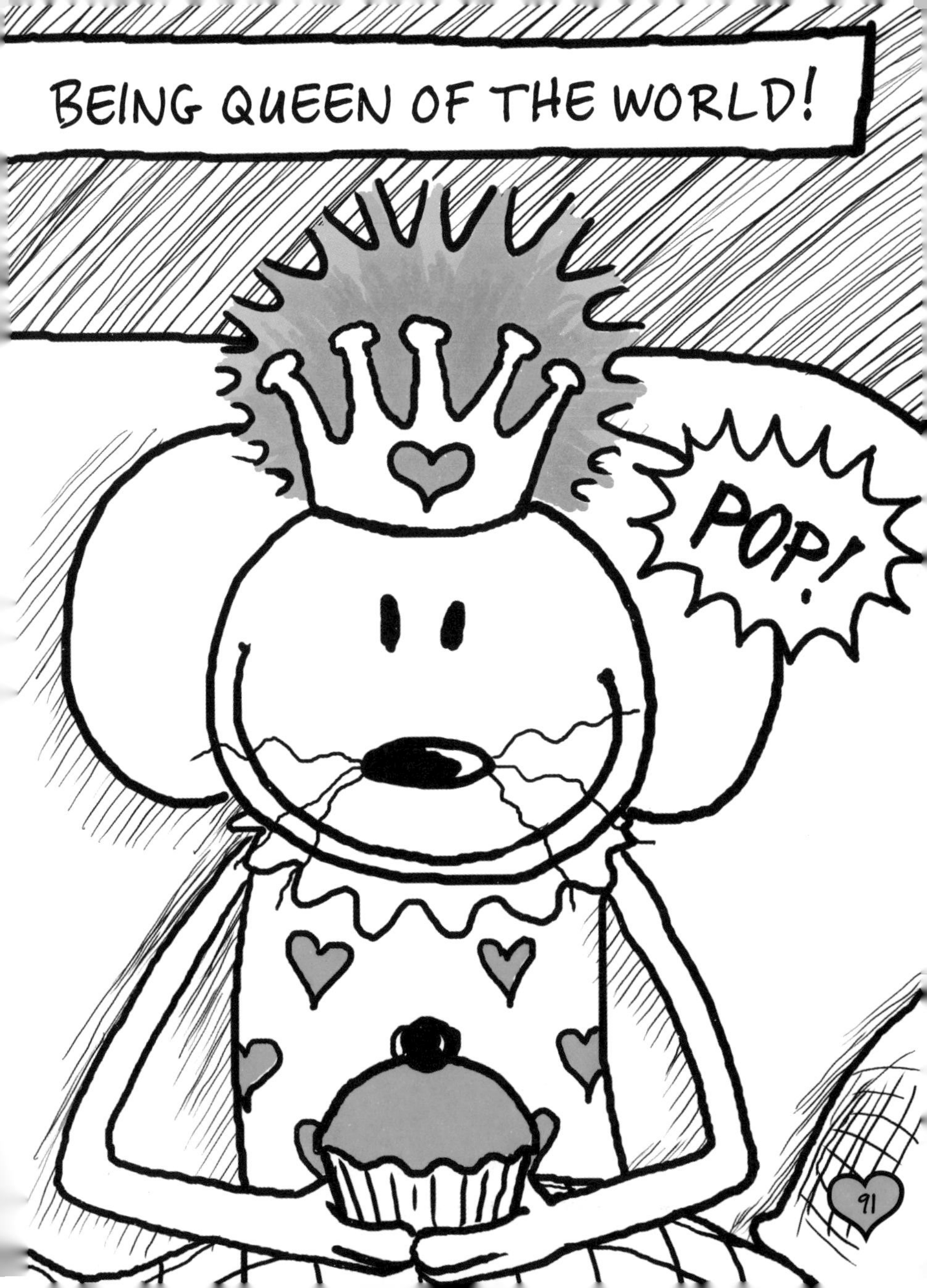
BEING QUEEN OF THE WORLD!
POP!